Creation of the World What Children Ask and How God Would Answer

A Bible Story for Children

Deborah Kathleen Elizabeth Scott

AuthorHouse™
1663 Liberty Drive
Bloomington, IN 47403
www.authorhouse.com
Phone: 833-262-8899

Because of the dynamic nature of the Internet, any web addresses or links contained in this book may have changed
since publication and may no longer be valid. The views expressed in this work are solely those of the author and do
not necessarily reflect the views of the publisher, and the publisher hereby disclaims any responsibility for them.

Any people depicted in stock imagery provided by Getty Images are models,
and such images are being used for illustrative purposes only.
Certain stock imagery © Getty Images.

This book is printed on acid-free paper.

ISBN: 978-1-4259-5001-9 (sc)

Print information available on the last page.

Published by AuthorHouse 06/09/2022

authorHOUSE®

The author, dedication is in "Loving Memory" of her cousin "Butchie" John Henry Jackson Jr. who went with "GOD" to his "Kingdom" in 1965 at the age of 7."

Contents

Forward From The Author   v

About The Writing Author   vi

Creation of the World Day One   5

Creation of the World Day Two   7

Creation of the World Day Three   9

Creation of the World Day Four   11

Creation of the World Day Five   13

Creation of the World Day Six   15

Seventh Day of Rest for 'God'   19

Questions & Answers By 'God' & Children   21

Forward From The Author

Deborah had an idea about writing a book with a C.D that is available with voices that could be heard as well as read, on children understanding the "Bible" in their terms because of listing to her grandchildren in speaking of church, and how bored they get because they do not understand the concept of the "Bible" in adult terms. And wondered what children would ask "God" if they had a chance and how would he answer. Then she asked her grandchildren and other children what they though about it, and amazing enough they would ask "God" questions if they had a chance to, and would learn more from something they could understand in their terms. Then she asked the children some questions as to what they would ask "God" if they had a chance to about the creation of the world! Question were written down, and compiled together with the answers from the "Bible", and definition of words in the dictionary put everything together in the children's term. Then added the voices and musical C.D came up with;

"Creation Of The World What Children Ask And How Would God Answer", for children age's five to eleven.

The CD is available through my e-mail
LAZYDKS@aol.com

About The Writing Author

Deborah Kathleen Elizabeth Scott born December 2, 1949 in New Jersey and was raised in Philadelphia Pennsylvania and relocated over three decades ago to Northeastern Pennsylvania, and lives in a small town where her family ties go back to the late sixteen hundreds.

Being mother of three children that are all currently in the medical profession, and is a grandmother of six. She is daughter of the late Emaret Dorothy "Rozelle" Jackson her famous saying to Deborah was; "You can be anything you want to be", "God" gave you a gift use it! And believed she would be a good investigative writer.

She is a descendent of Michael 'Shummacher' Shoemaker, which gave her the right to the entitlement of Daughters of America, Daughters of the American Revolution. She is also a descendent of Katura Tuttle of the Iroquois, and Sara Hunter of the Seneca tribes, and because of that heritage is a member of a regional chapter for Native American Indians.

She was educated in the Philadelphia and surrounding area school system, and graduated a Philadelphia modeling and charm school then continued her education as an adult in the Wyoming Valley.

For several years worked, and managed restaurant establishments, operated a limo, and driving service prior to becoming a qualified private investigator.

Her strong religious belief is "God" has guided her life, and has a plan for all of us, which is her cause of action on everything she does, and attends several different denominations of churches.

She is an active environmentalist and has been contributive towards the environmental cleanup for three decades.

During the nineteen eighties she was president and head advisor of the "Blue Knights Drum and Bugle Corps twirling Unit" that was awarded a Citation of Merit for the Muscular Dystrophy Association and was active member in Minnie football and baseball league her children were allfiliated with.

At the present donates her time to the little league fundraisers, belongs to the Multiple Scorosis Society and is recognized for her support for the veterans of foreign wars. She is the Author of the autobiography "Are We Living In A Third World Country" in 1995. And is being considered for a nomination because of her writing.

Her future plans are to write several more books for children.

Her past time and hobbies include working on her house, dancing, music, swimming, water-skiing, ice skating, bowling, sewing, cooking, football, playing and teaching her grandsons baseball, and swimming. Traveling to different beaches with her sister Karen because of their love for the ocean, and meeting new and different people.

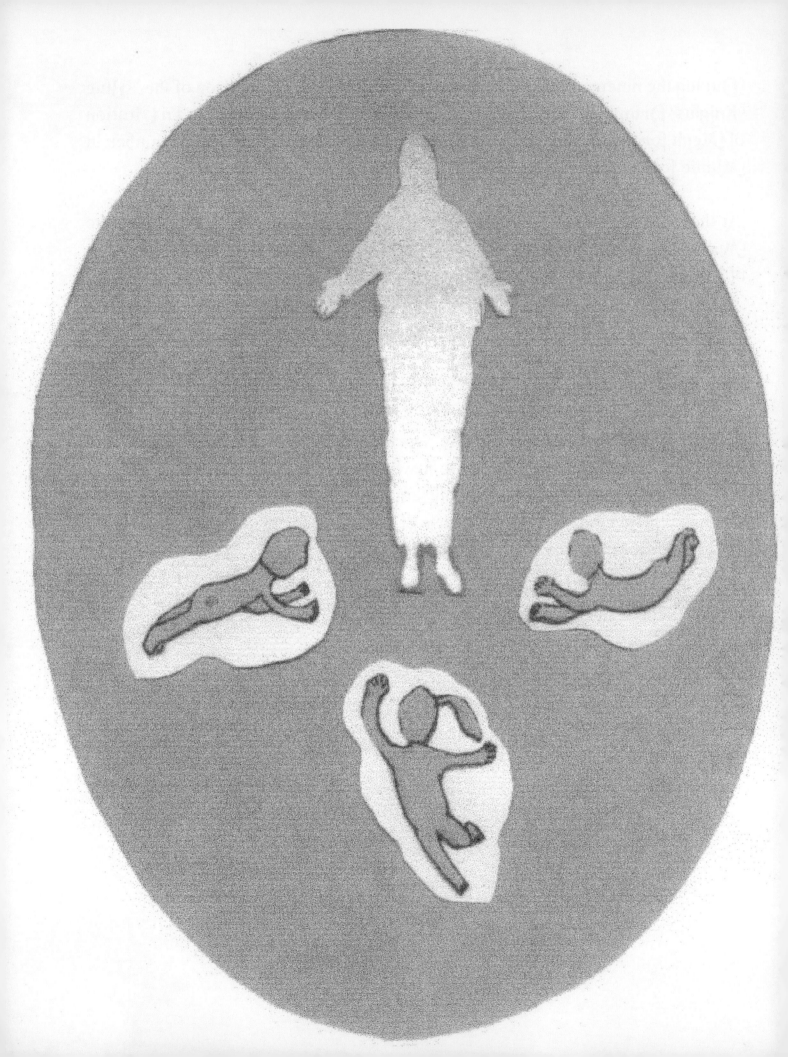

Creation Of The World What Children Ask And How God Would Answer

"Three floating spirits of children" are about to hear a voice! "A voice" of a spirit, who is going to explain the creation of the world! By "God" that is written in his book the "Bible"

'My children "I want, you to listen carefully and watch closely to see what "I am going to do". If you have any "questions" you may ask them of me and "I will answer.

A voice of a "Spirit Child" will answer with a question.

Oh! I have a question, "Who Are You?"

A voice will answer back by saying:

I"m "God", the spirit that is going to create the earth, the world, man, woman, all living and nonliving things.

The voice of the "Spirit Child" questions again:

It sounds like a lot of things your gonna create, and your gonna do it all by yourself?

The "Spirit Voice" of "God" answers!
Yes! It is a lot to create the world but "I alone, will do this.

Child - Wowwwwww !! "God" how can you do that?

God - Because I am "God" the one and only "God".

Child - Why can't we see you?

God - Because you must have faith in me and if you do that, you will always see me.

Child - "God" what is "Faith?"

God - Faith children is trust, word of honor in something you cannot see.

Child - Word of honor "God?"

God - Word of honor means, if I say I am going to do something "I will, do it! And even though you cannot see me, you will do what "I say, because "I am God.

Child - Ohhhhh!! HUMMMMMMMMMMMM "I Seee".

Child - "God" why is it so dark here?

God - It won't be dark for long, the first thing I am going to do, is create light! so my children can see all of my creations when "I'm done.

Child - Well what is light "God?"

God - You will see.

Child - "God" how long will it take to do all of your creations?

God- It will take six days and on the seventh day "I will, rest.

Child - What does days mean "God?"

God - I will explain it all to you in time children.

Child- Ok! That is why we have to listen and watch right "God?"

God - Yes! You will understand everything I am going to do.

"And So It Begins."

"The Six Days Of The
Creation Of The World".

" The Seventh Day of Prayer".

"By "God" Seen Through The
Eyes Of The Children".

First Day

"God" moved upon the waters and said, "Let there be light" and so it was.

The children saw brightness for the first time and were amazed to see what "God" had done.

Child– "WOWWW" that is cool, is that light "God?"

God– Yes! But "I am going to call it day, and the "darkness" from which you came will be "night", there will be "seven days" of light, and "seven nights" of darkness.

Child– Neattt! Coollll! OOH! But now we can see each other, how come we look so different "God"?.

God– You will see when "I am finished its part of my plan for all of my creations to look different from one another.

Child– "God" why do you call us children?

God– Because you are pure, innocent and you don't know good or evil! You are taught these things by your "Mother and a Father".

Child– How do we get a "Mother and Father" to know what good and evil is?

God – A "Mother and Father" will be part of my creation, sooo; you must pay attention and understand everything "I say, and do remember, "I am "God" the creator of all things.

The Second Day

God spoke to the children and said, "I am now creating the world a place "I will call my "Kingdom", if you lookup "I have made the sky "I will call my "Heaven". If you look down you will see dry land. "I will call "earth". "I will put grass, fruit, and trees with seed to make them grow, and all the waters "I will call seas".

"I want all of my children to know that "I God and "I alone, have created these things that are all good, and "I can take it all away from anything that is bad or evil.

Child– "God" what will you do with all you have created?

God– I am not finished yet children "I will, tell you later.

Child– Ok I can't wait.

Child– Nahhhh me either "God".

Child– "The Sky" you created is SOOOO; pretty "God".

Child– It's SOOOOO BIGGGGG! "How big is it?"

God – "The Sky" is bigger then my children can see it goes around the "Earth".

Child– "The Earth" is big too, right "God?"

God– Yes "I know, it will be filled with all "I have created things that please me".

Child– But! "God" what will the grass, fruit and trees do?

God – They will be life for my creations to feed upon.

Child– But! What does that mean?

God – These are things that my children and creatures will eat.

Child– Ohhhhhh! I see!

The Third Day

"God" decided on the third day "light" was not bright enough to see his creation and to make things grow, soooooo: he made a brighter "light" and the "sun" was created. And the "darkness" became brighter at "night" so the stars could sparkle and shine. "God" wanted to divide up the "days" and the "nights" so four signs were given for the four seasons, and the "days" became a "year".

God– So children, what do you think?

Child– "God" it's all soooooo pretty and neat thanks for letting us watch.

God– I want you to see all of this because "I want you to know that "I am, the one and only "God" that can do all of this even though you cannot see me.

Child– You are the creator of all of these things that will be in your kingdom right "God"?

God– Yes, children that is right.

Child– Why did you create a brighter light "God?"

God– To shine brighter on the heaven and sky and to have the fruit, trees and grass grow stronger.

Child– Ohhhh! I got it.

Child– What does the four seasons mean "God?"

God– A brief time when things must change to have winter spring, summer and fall.

Child– Well what is a year?

God – It is a number of days to have the four seasons.

Child– "WOWWWW!" that will be a lot of days.

Fourth Day

"God" wanted the seas to be filled with "creatures" that could live in the waters, and birds to fly high in the sky! He created the great whales and creeping creatures. And so it was done! After "God" was finished creating them, he saw it was good and he blessed all of them by saying increase and multiply.

The Children were looking in amazement and wonder of the creations that "God" would do these things for them. One child had so much excitement, and transferred his energy to the other "children".

Child–   "WHOOOOOOO!"

Child–   "WOW!" "COOL!".

Child–   "How Neat".

Child–   "God" I am so glad you let us watch.

God–   Thank you children, I want you to see these things because I want you to know that "I am "God" of heaven, earth, and all creations and "I can do anything, and these are the things that please me.

Child–   "God" why did you bless your creatures, and what does it means?

God–   It means, I gave my approval, it's what makes me happy, and they are sacred to me".

Child–   What does increase and multiply mean?

God–   Remember when I put the trees, grass and fruit on the earth with seed?

Child–   Yep! sure do.

Child–   "AHAAAAA" Ok.

Child–   "That was neat".

God–   It means, I wanted to see more of everything "I have created and the seed is what makes all things grow, so I have put a seed inside everything, "I have created".

Child–   " AHAAAA! I see!

11

Fifth Day

"God" wanted living things to roam on the land with cattle and creeping things that had four feet were created "creatures, and he called them "beast of the earth". The children were bewildered by the sight of these creatures and had more questions to ask "God".

Child– "God" why do these things look so different, they are walking all around are they children too?

God – They are part of life "I have created, and no! they are not "children" they are "beasts of the earth".

Child– Ohhhhh! Ok! "God" aren't you tired yet?

God – I never get tired and besides I am, not finished with my creations yet! I have one more day to go and then "I will rest".

Child– You mean there is more?

God – Yes child, there is more "I have to create someone in my image, to take care of all I have created". Someone you can see as well as hear. Someone who can teach all of "my children" about me, "God the Father" the creator of all living things.

Child– Ohhhh! I can't waittttt.

Child– That's gonna be the "Father and Mother" right "God?"

God – "Ahaaaaa" I see you are paying attention Yes, it will be a "Mother and Father".

Child– Does that mean we will see you too "God?"

God – No! Remember when I told you about "Faith"?

Child– Oh yah! that's right we don't have to see you, all we have to do is trust in you, your word and you will always be with us.

God– Yes! You understand.

Sixth Day

God wanted to create someone in his image he created man. He needed man to be able to multiply, so he created woman with seed, they were humans with living souls, and were different from each other, they were given more then any other of "Gods" creations.

"God" took the dust from the "Earth" and gave it the breath of life, and man became alive with flesh and bone. "God" called this man "Adam". A rib bone was taken from him, and of that same breath of life a woman was created, "God" called her "Eve". "God" wanted them to multiply and have children, and their "children" will call them "Mother and Father.

"God" parted the land and the waters into four sections, and made a special place for them, he called it the "Garden Of Eden". In this garden "God" put a special tree, "The tree of Knowledge". "God" forbade them to eat the fruit of this tree, because if they did then they would know bad and evil! "God" wanted his "Kingdom" pure and his children to live without sin! but most of all to obey his rules. If they obeyed him they would live in the "garden" with him and never die. There also was another creature called a "Serpent", it was deep in a hole in a field and lived in a place of unhappiness. The serpent was different from "God". It was evil, with an evil spirit, impure and knew only bad things, and wanted "Adam and Eve" to disobey "God".

There are many things that will be learned from "Adam and Eve" the bad, and evil that was taught to them by the serpent because they ate from the fruit tree of knowledge.

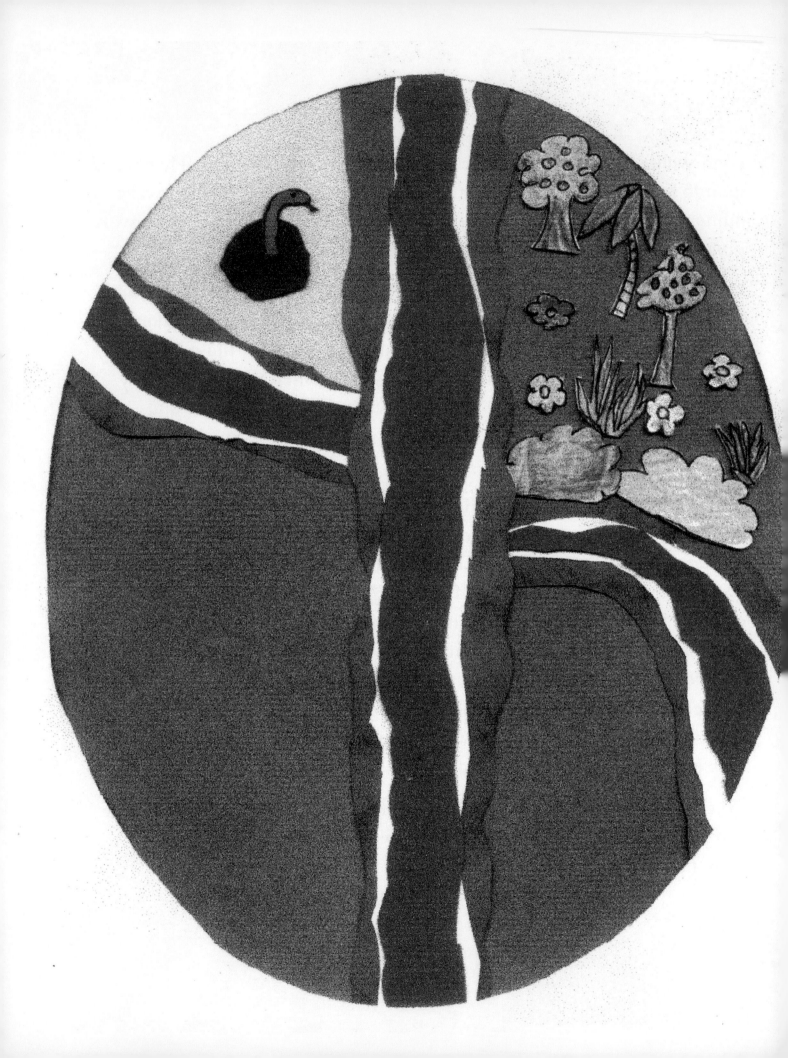

Child– "I understand, you made a man and a woman to become alive because you are "God" and you can do anything! Buuuuut! what does living soul mean?

God– It means! man will be able to see, feel, hear, smell and taste the five senses in all good things" "I have created, as long as they obey me! Then they can be with me in my "Kingdom".
The "Soul" is a "Spirit" you cannot see, and when the flesh, and bone of man and woman no longer live, they will come back to me, the earth where "I created man, and the soul will come back to me if they believe in me, and obey me" and live forever with me in my "Kingdom".

Child– Oh! I seeee!

Child– So the soul like you "God" we won't be able to see! but as long as we have "faith" in you and believe in you the "soul" goes back to you because you created man?.

God– Yes! That's what its means.

Child– But "God" what about all of the other things you created do they have a souls too?.

God– No! they don't.

Child– Uh hua, "I see, because they don't know good and evil like the "serpent" right "God?".

God– That's right! You are "understanding".

Seventh Day

On the seventh day it was quiet and the children were puzzled. They were talking to each other.

Child– Hey I don't hear "God" today! Where is he?

Child– I don't know lets ask!

Child– Helloooo! "God" are you thereece?

God– Yes! Children, "I am here.

Child– Are you making any more creations today?

God– No children, "I'm not, remember when "I told you it would take "six days" to make all my creations?

Child– "Oh yeaaaaaa".

Child– That's right!

God – Well then you should also remember "I told you, on the "seventh day" I will rest.

Child– Oh yea! Because you arc tired right "God"?

God – No child, I am never tired "I am, "God" "I want, the "seventh day" to be "Sanctified" for me.

Child– Hum, what? SANCTFFFFFFFIED? We don't know, what that means "God?".

God– "I will explain, "I want you to listen very closely and remember this day is to be a "Holy Day" of devotion and pray for me, "God" for all I have created for mankind, to multiply with children, and to teach them that "I am, the one and only "God". The only things I ask of them is to abide by my rules and don't bring evil to my "Kingdom" and have a "Holy Day of Faith" just for me. If they do these things, then they shall be rewarded by me to live in my "Kingdom" forever.

Child– "I know, I wanna be with you "God".

Child– Me too! I don't want to live in a place of unhappiness like the "serpent". "I will, do all you ask "God".

After The Seventh Day Of Creations

Everything stopped and you could hear the sounds of "Gods" creations the water with waves of calm, and the birds singing with harmony as they flew across the sky, and the beauty of nature that echoed peace, and happiness through out the world that "God" had created with perfection, and he was pleased. The children were still curious about some things and wanted to ask "God" more questions.

Child–   Hey! "God" are you still there?

God–   Yes children, "I'm here don't you remember, I told you "I will always be here as long as you have "faith" in me".

Child–   Yea "God" we remember, but we want to talk some more is that Ok? We have faith "God".

Child–   Yea, we sure do!

Child–   I wanna be with you "God" 'I will, have a holy day for you.

God -   You can talk to me anytime you want to, what do you want to talk about?

Child–   Welllllllll, "God" we have more questions.

God -   Ask anything you want to and "I will answer".

Child -   You made "Adam and Eve", soooo; they are the first real Mother and Father?

God -   Yes they are.

Child–   Is that why you made them grown up? so they could have "children", to teach their "children", to have faith in you, and all you created? And on the "seventh day" you want them to show you how much they love you, by having "a holy day" just for you, and do all good things to make you happy?

God -   Yes, that is exactly what "I mean.

Child–   Gee! "God" that is not so hard to do, we think the things you created are neat.

Child–   Yea! "God" you worked so hard with making the earth, world and everything, I know, "I want to stay with you".

Child–   "I know, I will do everything you ask.

Child–   Yea! So will I "God".

Child–   I don't want to have knowledge of evil because, "I don't want to do bad things".

Child–   "God" do you have a "Mother and Father"?

God–   No! "I don't need one, I'm "God" the creator of "Adam and Eve" the first "Mother and Father" of the world.

Child–   How long will mankind live?

God–   Until "I decide, if they are worthy enough to be with me".

Child–   Will all the living souls go to you "God"?

God–   No because, some will do evil things against me and my "Kingdom", and will not believe in me.

Child–   Where do the souls who do evil against you go?

God -   They will go to another place, a place of unhappiness.

Child–   What happened to "Adam and Eve"?

God -   Well remember the tree of knowledge that would teach them bad and evil? And when "I told "Adam and Eve" not to eat the fruit from it?

Child–   Yeaaaaaaaa.

God -   And the "Serpent" that was different from me?

Child–   Yeaaaaaaa.

God -   Well the "Serpent" told "Eve" to eat the fruit from the tree because she would be like me! Well, she ate from the tree and told "Adam" to do the same, and he did so; I told them they had to leave the "Garden".

Child– But why was that bad?

God – Because they "disobeyed" me, they broke my rules, and evil entered my "Kingdom" it was no longer pure, so for that they had to punished.

Child– But no body could be like youuuu! You are "God" the one and only "God".

Child– But how did you punish them?

God – Remember the five senses, taste, see, feel, hear and smell?

Child– Yessssss!

God– Well when they were in the garden they only had good feeling's with the five senses but, when the "Evil Serpent" entered the garden they listened to that spirit instead of me "God", they learned bad and evil, they disobeyed me, and because "I am "God" "I had, to cast out all evil things from my "Garden" my "Kingdom".

Child– Ahaaaaaaaaaaaaaa, "I see.

Child– Did Adam and Eve have children?

God – Yes they did.

Child– Did they live in the "Garden"?

God – No because of what "Adam and Eve" did.

Child– OHHHHHHH! I see. They disobeyed you?

Child– How long will the world last?

God – Forever!

Child– If the world will last forever does that mean, heaven will last forever too!

God– Yes!

God – Are there any more questions Children?

Child– Naaaaa, not for now anyway "God".

Child– We know we can talk to you anytime "God" you will always be with us.

Child– Thanks "God" for explaining everything to us.

Child– Grown up's, go figure! that was sure dumb thing Adam and Eve did! "I know, I will always do what "God" says, I believe in him.

Child– Yeaaaa me too! "I know, I believe in him too".

Child– "God" didn't ask for much, all he wants is for his children to have "Faith" believe in him, have a "Holy Day" to thank him for all he created, obey him and do good things instead of bad things.

And we will be rewarded with "God" in his "Kingdom" Forever.

Printed in the United States
by Baker & Taylor Publisher Services